A Plane for Zane

T0337596

Written by Susannah Reed
Illustrated by David Hurtado

Collins

Who's in this story?

Listen and say

Lucy

Download the audio at www.collins.co.uk/839747

Tom

Zane

Tom says, "Hello, Lucy."
Lucy says, "Hi, Tom. Come in."

Tom asks, "What are you making?"
Lucy says, "A plane for Zane."

Tom asks, "Who's Zane?"

Lucy says, "Zane is my new toy robot. He's very clever. He can walk and talk."

Lucy says, "Zane wants to fly."

Zane can't fly. But he can fly in a plane!

Lucy says, "This is Zane's plane."
Tom says, "It's beautiful!"

Lucy finishes the plane.
She is very happy.

Lucy says, "Look at Zane's plane."
Tom asks, "Can it fly?"

Lucy takes Zane and his plane into the garden.

Lucy says, "Let's fly the plane, Zane!"

Lucy throws the plane.
It doesn't fly.

Oh, no!

Tom says, "Oh, dear! I'm sorry, Lucy."

Lucy says, "I know. Let's go to the park."

Come on, Tom!

Tom asks, "Where are we going?"
But Lucy doesn't answer.

Lucy and Tom are at the pond.
Lucy says, "Look at Zane now!"

Zane hasn't got a plane, but he's got a great boat!

Picture dictionary

Listen and repeat

boat

fly

garden

plane

pond

robot

throw

1 Look and order the story

2 Listen and say

Collins

Published by Collins
An imprint of HarperCollins*Publishers*
Westerhill Road
Bishopbriggs
Glasgow
G64 2QT

HarperCollins*Publishers*
Macken House, 39/40 Mayor Street Upper,
Dublin 1
DO1 C9W8
Ireland

William Collins' dream of knowledge for all began with the publication of his first book in 1819.

A self-educated mill worker, he not only enriched millions of lives, but also founded a flourishing publishing house. Today, staying true to this spirit, Collins books are packed with inspiration, innovation and practical expertise. They place you at the centre of a world of possibility and give you exactly what you need to explore it.

© HarperCollins*Publishers* Limited 2020

10 9 8 7 6 5 4 3

ISBN 978-0-00-839747-0

Collins® and COBUILD® are registered trademarks of HarperCollins*Publishers* Limited

www.collins.co.uk/elt

British Library Cataloguing in Publication Data

A catalogue record for this publication is available from the British Library.

Author: Susannah Reed
Illustrator: David Hurtado (Beehive)
Series editor: Rebecca Adlard
Publishing manager: Lisa Todd
Product managers: Jennifer Hall and Caroline Green
In-house editor: Alma Puts Keren
Project manager: Emily Hooton
Editor: Emma Wilkinson
Proofreaders: Natalie Murray and Michael Lamb
Cover designer: Kevin Robbins
Typesetter: 2Hoots Publishing Services Ltd
Audio produced by id audio, London
Reading guide author: Emma Wilkinson
Production controller: Rachel Weaver
Printed and bound in the UK by Pureprint

MIX
Paper | Supporting responsible forestry
FSC www.fsc.org
FSC™ C007454

This book contains FSC™ certified paper and other controlled sources to ensure responsible forest management.

For more information visit: www.harpercollins.co.uk/green

Download the audio for this book and a reading guide for parents and teachers at www.collins.co.uk/839747